FOUNDATIONS OF LOVE

A HARTS SQUARE PREQUEL

WALTER H. HOPGOOD

LISA D. WITTE

SQUIDGIEWITTY LLC

.

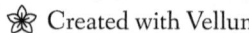

CHAPTER 1

KEELAN LOOKED over the parcel of land stretching out before him, predominantly green with splotches of yellow and pinks from the sunrise spilling across the horizon. He smiled, seeing beyond overgrown weeds studded with jagged pieces of concrete and broken beer bottles to how he would build his part of the American dream, just like his adopted parents had. He saw his future.

"It's beautiful, isn't it?"

Layte, his best friend and business partner, leaned into him and laughed with delight. He turned to see her shaking her head with a gently mocking expression.

"While this will indeed be a great future for us both," she said, maintaining her majestic demeanor even as a raccoon scurried into a nearby storm drain, "it is currently very much *not* beautiful." She released his arm as he looked back out over the field. "But you have always been a dreamer. It's one of the things I've always loved about you."

Love. That four-letter word that people used so easily. He and Layte had once been lovers, but that felt like two lifetimes ago. They'd known each other since childhood, but only started dating senior year of high school. And before graduation, their time as a couple stumbled to an end when Layte helped him accept the truth about himself.

She had cupped his cheek and fixed her rich brown eyes on him with a knowing smile. "You need to look into your heart, and honor your true nature."

Keelan had blustered, blushing from the knowledge that she must have figured out the secret he'd never even admitted to himself, much less spoken of to anyone. The secret that he'd planned to keep forever, because his Dad always said 'tradition is the foundation of every part of your life', and how could he follow family traditions when he's anything *but* traditional?

But, eventually, with his best friend's support and encouragement, he accepted his sexuality and came out. He'd never figured out how Layte knew he was gay before he'd even come to grips with it himself, but whenever he asked, she just smiled and shook her head fondly.

During their college years, Layte and Keelan grew to be closer as friends than they had been as lovers.

Forgoing the usual college path, Layte refused to declare a major. Instead, she took any and every class that interested her, from engine repair to business management to psychology. After graduation, she used her enormous variety of skills to start her own business as a 'Jill of All Trades'. She also spent hours as a ride-share driver whenever her schedule permitted, because she 'wanted to meet people from all walks of life'.

Keelan took a more traditional path, and followed his father, Arthur Greene, into architecture. He interned at the family firm all through college, and was hired upon getting his degree. He started off doing 'entry-level' projects like courtyards and office buildings, but after several years his soul longed to do more creatively fulfilling designs. Watching Layte succeed at challenge after opportunity lit a fire in him to take a risk and spread his wings, and now it seemed like he was about to get his chance.

*
**

One lazy Portland afternoon a few weeks back, Keelan and Layte headed out to run errands and have dinner. Driving down Southeast Stark Street with the setting sun at their backs, they passed a parcel of land that featured in Keelan's fondest childhood memories. Before those memories could distract him, he saw an elderly man tamping a sign into a bit of dirt. The car slowed, and he turned to see that Layte had noticed him, too.

Layte was already pulling over onto the gravel verge, and they watched the old man turn, his shoulders stooped, and slowly walk past a gas station that had closed and crumbled decades before.

"Is it really finally for sale?" Keelan kept his eyes on the retreating figure. "I used to play in that lot when I was a kid."

"As did I," Layte replied. "I believe this is one of the places where our paths crossed before we really got to know each other." Sometimes Keelan forgot they had lived so near to each other, and even spent time in the same circles, because they hadn't gotten close until high school.

Keelan smiled at memories of his friends, carefree as a group of six year olds could be, until the old man turning down a gravel driveway caught his eye. He glanced at Layte, his thoughts racing. "Then that... No, it *couldn't* be! You don't suppose that's Old Man Hart, do you?"

Layte put the car in park, and Keelan was out before she could answer. "Excuse me?" he called out. When the elderly man didn't turn, Keelan jogged to catch up. "Excuse me. S*ir?*"

Layte caught up just as the elderly man stopped and slowly turned. As dark, soulful eyes looked him and Layte up and down, Keelan felt like he was six years old all over again. He knew those eyes, though it had been decades since he'd seen them. His tongue twisted in his mouth with unasked questions, but Layte found her voice first.

"Excuse me, sir, but you wouldn't happen to be Jacob Hart?"

A smile bloomed on the elderly man's face, forming laugh lines that cemented Keelan's recognition. "I remember you. You used to live," he said, "down at the yellow house at the end of the block."

"Yes, sir," she replied with a smile. "My name is Layte. And this is Keelan. He used to live here as well, about two blocks over."

Mr. Hart turned sharp eyes on Keelan. "Oh, the Greene's boy." With a nod, he added. "Your momma made a fine pot of stew for us when we lost our boy Hunter a few years back."

Keelan smiled, because that sounded exactly like

his mother. His parents still lived in the house they'd brought him home to nearly three decades ago.

Mr. Hart's smile turned sad, and Keelan saw his eyes shining. Whatever memories played in his head obviously brought him little comfort. Mr. Hart wiped away a tear, then nodded at Layte's car. "Looks like you two've grown up and done well for yourselves."

"Yes, sir," Keelan said, trying to remember a young man named Hunter from his youth. "I'm an architect, and Layte's good at just about everything. We were just talking about starting a business together. Actually, we were hoping to build a business park here in Southeast. You know how Portland keeps growing."

"Don't I know it," Jacob replied. "I've had people hounding me to sell this property for years, but I knew it just wasn't the right time." He turned to look at the property, Layte and Keelan joining him.

Keelan suddenly remembered a boy named Hunter who was about ten years older than him and his friends. They'd never really played together, being so far apart in age. If Hunter had died three or four years ago, he couldn't have been more than 40. That thought redoubled Keelan's determination to start a family – a legacy – of his own.

After sharing a look, Layte put a gentle hand on

Jacob's shoulder. "May we ask what made you change your mind?"

Mr. Hart nodded. "I was-" he started, but shook his head. "Tell you what. If you two really are interested in the property, grab that sign and come back to the house and talk." He turned and started walking.

It took less than a second for Layte to agree with a nod. Keelan ran to grab the sign as Layte caught up to Mr. Hart. "We would love to."

They followed Jacob to a small house that sat at the back of the property. It was well kept, but the décor was severely out of date, including dozens of delicate doilies adorning the chairs and tables. Still, touches of elegance surrounded them, from the crown molding to the intricate hand-stenciled border around the kitchen pass through. They reminded Keelan of his parent's place just a few blocks away, and spoke of it being a home, rather than just a house.

Settled around the kitchen table, Jacob asked Layte and Keelan what would be a fair price for the property. They conferred briefly, and then looked online for comparable business-zoned properties before settling on a price that was agreeable to them all.

Business over, they continued to visit in the quaint kitchen filled with hand-made touches. Jacob said that he could have sold the property to any number of developers, but his wife had always told him to hold off for the right people.

"Well, I was talking to my Lucy this morning, and decided that today was the day. And here you two are." He smiled warmly at them.

"Is she here?" Keelan asked.

"It has been many years since I have seen your wife, Mr. Hart," Layte added as she glanced around. "I would love to say hello."

"I, uh," Jacob started, then stopped, frowning. As the silence stretched between them, Jacob looked at his arthritic hands, wringing in his lap. Layte, with her uncanny sense of always knowing what was needed, grabbed a napkin from the porcelain holder in the center of the table. She handed it to Jacob, who dabbed at eyes suddenly rimmed with tears.

When he spoke, his voice was barely a whisper. "I lost my Lucy a few months back. Married sixty-five years. Our other son Kenneth wants me to move down to Eugene and live with him and his wife, but my life was here. With her. It's all I've known." He took a deep breath as he dropped the tear-stained napkin to the table. "I've been putting it off because it would mean closing that chapter of our lives together." He looked at Layte and then Keelan, forcing a smile. "I still talk to her, because even though she's not here, I know she's still with me."

He suddenly rapped his knuckles on the table with a genuine smile. "I don't care if my son thinks I'm crazy. Talking to her this morning got me to make that sign and put the property up for sale. And it got you two here, didn't it?"

Keelan smiled back, even as his heart broke a little. "Yes, sir, it did."

*
**

After the sale of the property was completed, Jacob told Layte and Keelan he'd be moving to Eugene to take his son and daughter-in-law up on their offer. Though Jacob had waved off their offer of help, a small army of people showed up to help him with the move, thanks to Keelan's parents putting out the word around the neighborhood.

While Keelan enjoyed helping the man who had given them space to play and let their imaginations run free, part of him ached to find the kind of love that Jacob and Lucy had shared for so many years.

Picking up a box with Layte, he looked askance at her knowing smile. "What?"

"For one of the most detail-oriented people I know," Layte said as they walked out into the warm

Portland afternoon, "you can be quite oblivious to what's going on around you."

Keelan looked around in confusion, seeing only neighbors helping out a man in need. "What am I missing?"

"That young man over there," she said, discreetly pointing to a mid-20s hipster with purple hair and blue eyes that seemed to follow Keelan, "and that handsome couple over there," she said, indicating a fortyish gay couple who both blushed when Keelan glanced their way, "have been, shall we say, sizing you up all morning."

Keelan knew he should loosen up and have some fun. He was only 34, after all. His Mediterranean background had gifted him with black hair, a light olive complexion, and green eyes, a combination that had inspired many admirers. But he'd been so focused on his part in the family legacy that the time never seemed right for romance, or even a quick fling. And now, with this multi-year project ahead of them, his love life was just going to have to wait.

Instead of reacting to the men she'd pointed out, Keelan turned it back on his best friend. "I don't see you with anyone, Layte."

She smiled at him triumphantly. "I've actually gone out on a few dates lately." When he gave her a questioning look, she added, "What do you think I was doing while you were at the office working until midnight every day?"

That was news to him. And even as he smiled, an irrational part of him felt a flicker of jealousy.

*
**

Two weeks after Jacob Hart moved to Eugene, Layte and Keelan went to City Hall to get the plans for their business park approved.

Keelan had no interest in the administrative side for a couple of reasons: it seemed to be nothing but a headache of bureaucratic red tape, and his father had a whole team who took care of all that. Layte, however, had pointed out that this was **their** project, not his father's, and insisted that they handle the entire process together, right down to all the boring minutiae.

As they waited in ugly vinyl chairs that hadn't been updated since the 1970s, the mundanity of it weighed him down, to the point where he wished for something – anything – interesting to happen.

The red tape was exactly as annoying expected, but what he hadn't counted on was the long-haired clerk with tattoos peeking from the sleeves of his crisp white shirt. The flirtatious looks he sent at

Keelan flustered him, parching his throat and requiring Layte do all the talking.

After what felt like hours, the handsome young man at the permits office sent them to the next office with two additional forms to fill out, and a scrap of paper with a phone number.

"I believe this is for you," Layte said with a smile as she handed over the number.

Flustered, Keelan shoved it in his pocket and then ran a hand through his closely shorn hair. "He was so *forward*," he said, trying (unsuccessfully) not to sound scandalized.

Layte rolled her eyes. "That might be just what you need, Keelan," she said as they entered the next office to find more of the same uncomfortable chairs.

Keelan blushed. Though it had been quite a while since he'd dated, much less slept with a man, he pushed the thought from his mind. There was a time when he thought he could have it all: the love of a caring man, a life of fulfilling work, and, of course, his friendship with Layte. His adopted father's voice suddenly popped into his head. "Tradition. You work hard to build tradition and a legacy," he had said on more occasions than Keelan could count. "The rest comes later."

"Tradition," Keelan whispered.

"Keelan?" Layte asked. It wasn't until he

searched her eyes that he realized he'd spoken out loud. Her delicate hand on his shoulder grounded him in the present. "Where did you go?"

Keelan just shook his head, pushing away the thoughts that had shaped his life since the day he'd been adopted. While the memories were welcome, they reminded him that he needed to push his happiness until some time in the future, after he'd established his own traditions and legacy.

"Garbage," he said randomly. At Layte's confused look, he said, "We have to ask about commercial garbage service."

Layte smiled. "I believe we have some time. But right now," she waved the forms in her hand, "we have these to take care of. Not to mention submitting the blueprints for approval."

Keelan looked up to see the handsome clerk who had assisted them before walk in. He winked at Keelan, then went behind the counter and began a whispered conversation with the young woman there. Both looked up and studied Keelan, making him blush.

"How about you take care of those, and I will go drop these off with the city planner's office?" Keelan bounced the tube holding the blueprints off his other palm. He gave her a pleading smile. "Deal?"

Layte's arched eyebrow told him that she saw

right through him, but chose not to call him out. "Shall we meet at the café downstairs when we're done?" Clearly he was going to hear about this later.

"I'll have your mocha chai waiting."

Keelan retreated from the office with a wink, as well as an involuntary glance at the young man whose hopeful expression fell as he left. He didn't let out the breath he was holding until he was safely behind the closed doors of the elevator.

*
* *

Peter Larkins walked out of City Hall holding his brand new contractor's license reverently, like the lifeline that it was. Portland was the latest city in the never-ending tour that was his life. Each time he started over in a different city or country, it was like being reborn, with a clean slate. He liked it even better if it was far away from the disapproving family that had sent him off to boarding schools when he was just a little kid, and then conversion camp when he'd dared to come out.

As an adult, Peter had hidden his sexuality (conversion unsuccessful) from his small-minded father long enough to learn the ins and outs of his construction business – the only interest they had in common. As soon as he'd amassed enough knowledge to lead his own large-scale projects, he'd abandoned him just like his father had done to his mother when he was a small child.

He moved from London to Glasgow for a project, and followed another to Edinburgh. That set up a pattern for the next decade – move to a city with a population of around half a million, get his license, take on a job lasting six to eighteen months, and move on again. It kept his life interesting without tying him down. It was also a way to follow in his father's footsteps without being under his thumb.

Three years ago, in Liverpool, one of the plumbers suggested that he try his hand in the United States, because he was running out of right-sized cities in the UK.

While New York City's fast pace and access to hundreds of possibilities (construction and men alike) was very appealing, he'd settled in Indianapolis. That only lasted until the first winter storm, when Peter realized that he 'wasn't built for this type of environment'. Luckily, the smallish project was only weeks from completion and a good friend took over for him. He was able to leave for the more hospitable climes of the West Coast. He found a few minor jobs in Fresno and Tacoma, but ended up living off his savings for far too long. Six weeks into a dry spell, someone said that 'Portland seems to always be growing.' He did some research and decided to make the move.

A week later, he had a hotel room in the up and coming Southeast district, and the only thing standing between him and a new job was an Oregon contractor's license. And he'd just fixed that issue.

He took a moment to bask in the warm afternoon sun before heading back to his hotel room to finish up several bids. Suddenly, somebody barreled into him and knocked the license out of his hand. He watched it land on the edge of the puddle of chai the guy had spilled. Peter recovered his balance and glared.

"Oi! Watch where you're going, wanker!"

He suddenly realized how good-looking the guy was. He was a few inches taller than Peter, with broad shoulders and very short, dark brown hair that somehow still managed to curl. He also had eyes the color of the lush forests Peter had seen out the train window on the ride down from Tacoma.

"Sorry, sorry," the man said. He juggled his two drinks, then snagged the license and shook off what liquid he could. Before Peter could say anything else, he'd thrust it into his hands and disappeared into the City Hall building.

Peter muttered "Shit," as his quick ire turned to lust. He shook the license again and wiped it on his pants leg before putting it in his back pocket. He off in search of the light rail line that would take him back to his hotel, and counted the days since he'd last touched a man. Maybe if he made quick work of the applications that awaited him, he'd be able to solve both problems in one afternoon.

Work and lust were two things Peter excelled at, while love was the farthest from his mind. Sure, he'd felt a spark with a couple of the men he'd hooked up with, but nothing that matched the urge to get back on the road, find a new project, and move on. His father had done it, so why shouldn't he? It didn't matter that he'd pretty much hated his father for never putting him first, and for sending him to boarding school so that someone else could deal with the troubles of a hormonal teenager. All that really mattered was doing what he wanted, the rest of the world be damned.

CHAPTER 2

KEELAN AND LAYTE spent the next two weeks getting their project off the ground: Keelan working with the city and Layte reviewing bids and interviewing prospective contractors. They already know their project would be a hit, as retail space was seriously lacking in outer Southeast Portland. If that wasn't assurance enough, multiple parties were already interested in signing leases – even before ground had been broken.

Sitting in his small office at his father's architecture firm, they plotted out their next steps.

"You do know that you will soon have to leave this place," Layte said as she set a folder in front of him.

Keelan knew it was true. In order to focus his attention on their project, he would have to leave his father's firm. His father already understood. In fact, he and Keelan's mother were silent partners, putting up a considerable sum to help the project get off the ground. Still, it was quite a step out of his comfort zone.

Keelan opened the folder, and smiled at the proposed naming and signage. Hart's Square. When Layte and he had worked on the name, the idea of paying homage to The Harts came up. When Keelan suggested Hart's Square, "Like two hearts entwined," everything just clicked.

Layte immediately agreed, and they believed the project was the beginning of their own legacy, while honoring Jacob and Lucy Hart who'd come before them.

"I've narrowed the project manager down to two candidates," she said, bringing his attention back to the matter at hand. "No doubt you'll recognize Samuel Edgecomb's name." She pulled the first proposal out of the pile, with his name circled in red marker.

Keelan was indeed familiar with Sam, since he and Keelan's father had been responsible for quite a few developments, including a spectacular revitalization of part of the waterfront. He was Keelan's choice, because he was safe. Traditional. And you didn't fuck with tradition.

Keelan made up his mind without even looking at the other profile. In his mind, he was already at the building site with Sam directing teams on various projects. But Layte quickly brought him back to the present when she pulled out a second bid. "This is from someone new to the area, but I believe it fits in quite well with what we're trying to do here."

Keelan saw 'Peter Larkins', circled in red marker and underlined twice. "Larkins? Never heard of him." He clicked his pen while he thought, then said, "Let me go ask Dad what he knows about him."

Layte sat up a little straighter, lifting one eyebrow. Keelan usually loved when she challenged him; she was generally right, and he was able to learn a lesson and become a better person. But this time, the eyebrow made him a little nervous.

"What?" Damn his voice for breaking.

"While I appreciate your father's wealth of knowledge, do you think it wise to rely on him when this is something that we are quite capable of doing ourselves?" She pulled her long hair back into a ponytail. "After all, isn't that why we started this project in the first place?"

Keelan realized that, once again, his friend was right. He took a deep, calming breath, and then let it go. "Very well. But it doesn't change who I would pick for the project."

After considering each other for a moment, they simultaneously revealed their answers.

"Sam." "Peter Larkins."

"Seriously?" Keelan asked. "He's a complete unknown. What does he even know about Portland?" Keelan looked over the list of projects Larkins had managed. "Liverpool. Glasgow. Fresno. Indianapolis. I mean, he's never even worked in Portland." He glanced at the paperwork again. "And he left Indianapolis before his project was completed! What if he decides to leave before *our* project is completed?" How on earth could they trust a possible flight risk with their legacy?

"I asked about that," Layte replied. "He said that he left early due to the extremely harsh winter. But it was only five weeks, he hired his own replacement, and the project still came in under budget."

"Well, what if he decides he doesn't like Portland because of the rain?"

Layte leveled her gaze at him. "I believe it rains more in London than it does here, Keelan."

He knew that arguing with Layte was fruitless. But as he opened his mouth to respond anyway, a memory tickled the back of his brain. Sam. Samuel Edgecomb. "Wait a minute, Sam announced his retirement six months ago," he said, crestfallen.

Layte had the audacity to lay a well-manicured

hand on her throat in an attempt to look innocent. "Did he? Well, I guess that makes our decision that much easier."

"How did his application even make it into the running, I wonder?"

His question was met with a smirk.

With a heavy sigh, Keelan asked, "So, when am I meeting with this *Larkins* character?"

Shortly after the work trailer was delivered to the property, and the power and water hooked up, Keelan was busy getting everything situated. This would be his and Layte's office for the foreseeable future, so he wanted it to be perfect for them. He didn't mind sharing with her, but wasn't as sure about the new project manager. The one Layte had already hired, so meeting him was just a formality.

Larkins was the last piece of a puzzle that already spanned half a dozen companies. He was arguably the most integral, since he would have to coordinate all of the sub-contractors and projects, juggling multiple priorities. Neither he nor Layte had experience at that, or aspired to learn. Larkins's experience would perfectly complement their strengths.

A knock on the door brought him out of his thoughts, so he put a thumbtack into the plan on one of the many corkboards (the opposite wall covered in whiteboards for brainstorming), and opened the door to find a handsome man who looked to be in his 30s, with dark, well-styled hair, dark, soulful eyes, and lips that...

"Hello?"

The English accent jolted Keelan out of his reverie. He waved the newcomer in, temporarily struck mute by the enchanting man walking into the trailer.

"Peter," he said, holding out a hand. "Peter Larkins." After a long moment where Keelan didn't respond beyond taking his hand, Peter continued, "And you must be Keelan?"

"Keelan, yes." He felt his face warm, and knew he was blushing. He shook his head, as if to reboot his brain. "Sorry, sorry. You caught me, uh..." But that's all he got out, because his libido had taken over his higher functions.

"Daydreaming?" Peter offered.

Keelan shook his head as he finally released Peter's hand. "No, no, sorry." He pointed to the board where the project blueprints were pinned. "Contemplating."

"So, not at all like daydreaming," Peter said, with

a smirk.

They both smiled, and then burst out laughing.

"Sorry, sorry," Peter managed between breaths. "I don't mean to take the piss." When Keelan gave him a quizzical look, he added, "Make fun. I don't mean to make fun, as you Americans say."

At least *that* made sense to Keelan.

"No problem. It's very nice to meet you, Peter," he said, gesturing for him to take a seat. "This is the office we'll be working in. This is my desk, that's Layte's – you remember her, of course?"

"Oh, absolutely," Peter replied. "One of the most intense interviews I've ever gone through." He eased back into the chair and threw an arm over the back. "Tell me. Was she the easy one, or are you?"

Keelan, who'd just taken a sip, choked, spraying water on his new desk calendar.

"You okay there?" Peter asked, his look of concern quickly giving way to a smirk.

"Easy?" Keelan asked, as he wiped his calendar off as best he could.

"Yes," Peter clarified. "Was she the easy interview? Or are you the easy one?"

Keelan wasn't sure if this was just the divide between British customs and American ones, or if Peter Larkins was coming on to him.

"I guess you could say I'm the easier interview,"

Keelan finally said. Peter's only reply was a smile. "So, how about a tour of the property?"

"I'd love it, but I have a question before we start. I've never heard the name Keelan before. Where does it come from?"

Keelan hesitated, but not because he was ashamed of his heritage. It was people's follow-up questions that made him uncomfortable. "It's Greek," he said. "A very traditional Greek name."

"Ah, Greek," Peter responded. "I should have realized that, what with your olive complexion. Where in Greece is your family from?"

"Actually," Keelan said, stopping Peter before he could dig any deeper, "I'm not sure. My parents gave me up at birth. I take my heritage from my adopted family."

Peter looked a bit embarrassed. To avoid further awkwardness, Keelan stood up and got ready to leave, with Peter following his lead. "Shall we?"

Halfway to the door, Keelan stopped and went back for his phone. He averted his eyes to avoid staring at the polo stretched across Peter's arms and chest. "Hang on. We should exchange phone numbers."

Peter's smirk reappeared, and his nutmeg brown eyes sparkled with humor. He was two or three inches shorter than Keelan, but with thick biceps and broad shoulders that tapered down to a trim waist. He was exactly Keelan's type, not intimidated by Keelan's greater height and muscular enough to pick him up like he weighed nothing. Keelan's breath caught as he imagined it, and he felt himself blushing.

Keelan broke free of from the thought of being manhandled by Peter, and tried to cover. "You know, because we're going to be working together, so I'll need to get in touch with you."

"Gladly," Peter said. But instead of saying his number, he reached for Keelan's phone. The curl of his fingers around the phone nearly took Keelan's breath away. "May I?"

"Sure." He voice broke and he coughed a few times to try and cover it up as Peter added his contact information. But then Peter leaned back, took a selfie, and assigned it to his contact before handing the phone back. Keelan had no doubt his cheeks were a deep, fiery red.

*
**

Peter'd had concerns about working with first time developers, but the tour of the building site went very smoothly. They followed up with a detailed overview of the plans for the project, along with a thorough vetting of the contractors taking part. Because Peter was new to town, he needed to learn the idiosyncrasies of the local construction scene. Working closely with Keelan, who knew them all, only made sense if they were going to stay on schedule and in budget.

Besides which, he found it incredibly easy to flirt with Keelan, though he knew he shouldn't. Peter just couldn't seem to pass up a chance to see him get flustered. While Keelan was stunningly handsome, the project hadn't even broken ground yet, and he knew he needed to back off.

But a *little* flirting couldn't hurt anything, and fed a part of his soul.

One point that Keelan seemed to dwell on was *tradition*. It clearly meant something to him, and though Peter understood the sentiment, he couldn't quite relate. Yes, he'd temporarily become part of his father's legacy to learn what he needed. But he ditched the tradition that wouldn't accept him as he was in order to leave his own stamp on every patch of land he worked.

Peter's stomach growled loudly. "Sorry," he said, as he checked his watch. They'd been there for six hours. Six hours *just talking*. Peter'd had hookups last less than that. "I didn't realize it was so late."

"Oh, wow," Keelan said, glancing at the wall

clock. "No wonder the traffic stopped. Everyone's gone home already." He stretched, and Peter secretly hoped his button-down would pull free of his khakis to give him a peek at the figure underneath. Keelan seemed well built, with a solid frame, but his clothes were too baggy to really tell. Peter liked men who showed off their muscles with tight shirts outlining muscular backs that tapered to a tiny waist, and sleeves straining to contain big biceps. Keelan seemed to fit the bill exactly, except for his loose-fitting clothing. Maybe that could help Peter resist coming onto him further.

"Dinner?" Peter didn't want the day to be over. He wanted to linger, to make more memories he could take back to his hotel room, on the off chance he couldn't convince Keelan to actually come and play.

Keelan blushed again, and Peter couldn't help but smile. "Let me text Layte and see if she'd like to join us." Keelan glanced at his mobile, and Peter couldn't help his quick frown. He wanted time with just the two of them, but understood if Keelan wanted to include his business partner.

"There's a brewpub near my hotel. Von Eberts, I believe? I read about it on the train," Peter suggested. He'd eaten there when he first arrived in Portland, and had loved it. Plus, they had a wide selection wines that he wanted to try. He wasn't familiar with Pacific Northwest wines, though, so he'd ended up ordering a beer.

Some indecipherable expression flashed across Keelan's face. Peter couldn't read it, but it didn't seem promising.

Keelan held up his phone. "Layte's fixing her parents' transmission, so she can't join us."

Peter studied Keelan's face, but it was like a wall had gone up where his emotions had once been. What had he said? All he'd suggested was a restaurant near his hotel.

"Perhaps next time, then. So, shall I drive?" He stood and stretched, enjoying the warm play of his muscles after sitting for so long, then stepped toward to the door.

Keelan shook his head. "We'd just have to come back here for my car, and I live up in the Pearl."

"The Pearl?"

"It's a district in northwest Portland, adjacent to downtown."

"It sounds very nice," Peter said. "I'd like to see it sometime."

Keelan seemed to loosen a bit, but there was still something distant to his manner. "How about I close up shop here and meet you there in 30?"

Peter smiled. "Sounds like a plan."

CHAPTER 3

"WHAT AM I DOING?" Keelan asked himself. He'd closed up the trailer and secured everything at the building site when the words started running over and over in his head. "Even if he *was* flirting, I shouldn't be doing this."

Keelan unlocked his car, then looked over its roof at their brand new trailer. Its bright and shiny exterior was slightly unnerving, because he was used to his father's dusty and dented mobile offices. While this project was the start of making his own name, of building his own reputation, he also craved tradition. Ritual. Familiarity. This building site was filled with too much jarring newness, and it set his teeth on edge.

Getting in, Keelan grabbed his phone instead of starting the car. He pulled up Peter's contact, and was greeted with his smiling picture. That smile had stirred something in Keelan from the very start, but how could he trust that instant reaction? He and Layte had dated only after knowing each other for a long while.

Keelan typed out *Sorry, won't be able to make it* and hit the send button before he could overthink it. Feeling guilty, he immediately followed up with *Raincheck?*

The progress bubble popped up, then disappeared. Then it did it again – six or seven times. It bugged Keelan that Peter was taking so long to respond, but *Sure thing* eventually popped up on his screen.

Keelan ran his fingers through his hair and let out a sigh. How had Peter gotten under his skin so quickly? He had far too much to worry about with the project, and didn't have time for this. He finally started the car and left the jobsite, glancing at the darkened trailer in the mirror, thinking about the memories that it already contained.

A few minutes later, Keelan pulled up in front of his parent's house instead of getting on the highway. It's like he was on autopilot, and hadn't realized until he parked. He looked at the house, and remembered seeing it for the first time when he was six years old and fresh from a Multnomah County group house. It was dark then, too, but he'd had the comfort of his adoptive parents holding his hands, and his new mother Victoria saying, "This is where you're going to live now, Keelan."

Keelan hadn't known it at the time, but that was the start of his *real* life. The foster care system had taught him to rely only on himself, but Victoria and Arthur spent years proving that he could depend on them. And once he understood how important his father was to the city of Portland ("He knows the *mayor?* Wow!"), it helped shaped Keelan's worldview.

Even though it was late evening, he knew his parents were up. He could see the flickering light of a television changing channels every few seconds, undoubtedly due to his father. Keelan smiled, comforted by the familiar sight. Though some might call it mundane, he thought of it as stability. Keelan gave a quick knock and walked in, knowing the door would be unlocked. "Dad? Mom? I'm home!"

"Hey, son," Arthur Greene said from his favorite recliner, a present from Keelan for his 65th birthday. He hadn't been sure his dad would like it, and thought it might end up in the garage. Instead, it was soon joined in his parent's living room by a matching one for his mom. "What're you doing here? Not that your mother and I don't appreciate the visit."

Keelan dropped a kiss on the top of his father's head. "Hiya, dad." As he took a seat on the couch, he asked, "Where's mom?"

"It's her *alone time.* She's taking a bath."

"*Is that Keelan?*" came from the master suite down the hall. Though the house had felt enormous when Keelan was a child, it now felt tiny in comparison to his downtown loft. "*Did you eat dinner, honey?*"

"I'll take care of him," Arthur called back at the same time Keelan said, "I'm fine, mom!"

"Fine, my Aunt Fanny," Arthur said as he got out of his chair. Keelan quickly helped his father up. Arthur Greene didn't exactly *need* help, but it felt like the right thing to do. "Never *did* eat enough to get some meat on those bones," his father muttered.

"I'm fine, Dad," Keelan said as he followed his father into the kitchen. It held the small details that made a house a home; little touches of that reminded him of Jacob Hart's home, now sitting empty.

Arthur went to the refrigerator and starting pulling out containers. "Yeah, well, your mother and I didn't raise you just so you could starve yourself once you were on your own. I remember when you were barely higher than my knee. You never ate a proper meal the first two years after we brought you home."

Keelan just shook his head fondly, secretly enjoying the talk he got every time he came around past suppertime.

Before long, he was watching television with his father, an heaping plate of food on his knees and a glass of milk on the end table. *Milk*, when he'd had been drinking alcohol for over a decade. He figured it was one reason he sometimes still felt like that scared six-year-old when he was at his parent's house.

"So what's going on, son?" Arthur asked, clicking through a bunch of channels and stopping on a BBC show.

"Oh, Sherlock," Keelan said. "I've been meaning to watch this." He took a bite just as one of the characters said, 'Bloody wanker!' As the show continued, the words played over and over in his head. He'd heard them before... "That's where..."

"That's where what?"

Keelan shook his head as he wondered exactly how insulting the term 'wanker' was. "Nothing, nothing. It's just, the project manager that Layte hired – he's British." He wasn't throwing Layte under the bus, just happy to come up with a plausible diversion.

"British?" his father asked. "How long's he been in Portland?"

"Just a couple weeks. He's out here from... Well, just about everywhere, actually."

Arthur turned to look at him with sharp, steady eyes that Keelan had seen commanding fleets of construction workers on countless jobsites. While his gaze wasn't scolding, it did make Keelan feel younger than his years. "What can a man who's been in town all of a couple of weeks know about Portland? This isn't some big city where things go exactly how they're supposed to go. You've got to know people. You've got to build relationships. You've got to understand the foundation of the city before you can pour the foundation of a building."

Foundations. Arthur had built his life on that word. He'd instilled those same principles in Keelan and made him into the man he was today.

His mother walked in before Keelan could respond, dropped a kiss on Arthur's lips, and came over for a hug. "I'm so glad you stopped by," she said, smiling. "Here, let me get you some more." She reached his plate of barely-touched food.

"No, no, Ma, I'm fine. I'm still working on this," he said, taking a bite.

She studied him, then looked at Arthur, who shrugged.

"So, how is your project going?"

After visiting with his parents, and having two containers of leftovers pressed on him, Keelan got in his car and started driving towards the Pearl. The traffic was very light at 10 P.M., but he could see that he would be spending a lot of time in Southeast, on the opposite side of the city. That's not only where his father's firm was located, along with his parents' house, but also, the project.

He could also foresee late nights dealing with the inevitable emergencies that crop up and force plan revisions on even the most meticulously laid out projects. He'd seen it growing up, where his father might be gone for days at a time. But everything that his father had done, he'd done to set him on the right path in life.

That thought brought back one of his favorite – but at the same time, most horrific – memories of growing up. Just out of high school, he and his mother were going to buy supplies for when he moved to the dorms later that fall.

"I don't care who you settle down with," his mother had said. "A girl. A boy. *A couple-*"

"*Mom!*" he'd practically shrieked.

"Oh, hush," she'd said, clearly happy that she'd

scandalized her son. "I grew up in the '70s before all this puritan nonsense started."

Mercifully, his train of memories derailed before he could recall one of his mother's 'before I met your father' stories about allowing yourself to be free in your sexuality.

Luckily, coming out to his parents hadn't been much of an issue, though he'd worried it might. He'd kept his secret until just before his 18th birthday, figuring that if they reacted badly and abandoned him like his birth parents had, he would at least be able to support himself.

In the end, his mother just smiled and asked, "Have you met the Williams's boy, Devin? He came out his senior year in high school, too." Of course that had been nearly a decade earlier. He wasn't even done rolling his eyes before his mother added, "I know, I know. He's too old for you. But maybe he has friends who are your age."

That's one of the things Keelan loved about her — how much she cared. She cared enough to adopt a scared little boy who'd been shuffled around the foster care system since birth. And she cared enough to try to set him up multiple times — as long as he was happy.

His father's reaction was a smile and some shared tears, followed by his usual advice. "Build the foundation first. Once you have that, you can start to build your life on top of it."

Foundation. The word tumbled around in his head as he pulled onto I-84 and headed for downtown Portland. He'd always known that he needed to establish himself first, and then everything else would fall into place later. It's how he planned his life, and knew it was the best way forward.

A text lit up his phone in its dashboard holder. He gave a voice command, and the text was read out in a monotone. "From Peter Larkins. Message: Thank you for the introductions today. I have already been in contact with a few of the teams. Clearing will start bright and early on Monday, and we should be able to start carve-outs and foundation work the week next. Have a good night. End of message."

There was that word again – foundation. And while Keelan could totally see Peter's appeal – he was a stunningly handsome man – he couldn't see building a foundation with someone who had no roots *anywhere*.

They'd talked about how he'd learned from his father in England, but had taken his knowledge on the road. How do you build a life like that? Work with people for a year, maybe 18 months, and then just walk away? Keelan was still friends with people that he'd met the very week his parents brought him home. He still kept in touch with many of them, while Peter barely talked about friends, or even colleagues – just projects. Something he could conquer and then walk away from.

It was no way to live, at least for Keelan. Flirting or not, there was absolutely no way Keelan could ever see a future with someone like *that*.

CHAPTER 4

PETER SAT in his hotel room, partly hoping to get a reply from Keelan, and partly horrified at the prospect, because he'd remembered. Remembered that he'd called *Keelan* a 'bloody wanker'.

The day had started out quite relaxed. They'd had talked in the project trailer for hours, and Peter loved watching the blush bloom across Keelan's olive skin whenever he flirted with him.

Once back at his hotel, he'd jumped in the shower in case he was reading the signals properly. Though Keelan seemed flustered by the flirting, there was undeniably a spark as they exchanged phone numbers. Peter had thought he had a chance, even as the only advice his father ever gave him echoed in his mind. "Don't shit where you eat."

His father followed that advice to the letter.

They'd moved from town to town and project to project, never staying long. He'd hated it as a kid, because it meant that he never had close friends. As soon as he'd started dating, though, his nomadic life became an asset – he could meet someone, hook up for a while, and then move on to the next town. Just like his father.

He thought back to his dinner invitation, with all its implications. Sure, if Keelan had taken him up on it, the whole thing could have ended badly. But taking chances was what made life worth living. After all, he'd taken a chance by moving to America, and another coming to Portland.

If things didn't work out in Portland, there were plenty of cities in the United States where he could try again. Hell, he could even move back to England and start picking off his father's clients again, like he'd done with his first project in Glasgow. Proving himself to be worthy competition was the only way he'd gotten his father to respect him.

Still, there was something different about Keelan. Something that made Peter *feel* different. Peter wasn't used to having feelings attached to his sexual desires. A hookup was nothing more than two people scratching a mutual itch. His father had shown him that. After his parents split up, Peter had moved with his father to wherever the projects were. He'd seen his father find companionship in each town, then leave them once the project was over.

He'd often wondered what had become of his mother, but his father dismissed the question whenever it came up.

After Keelan had backed out of dinner, Peter went out on his own. He wanted to celebrate landing a job that paid him well to do what he loved. With the money he'd be socking away from this job, his retirement fund would be growing even faster than his projections. Living his life on the road, he didn't spend a lot on stuff that needed dragging around. Anyway, money in the bank was more important than possessions. Right?

He'd found a different brewpub, saving von Eberts in case Keelan ever took him up on his offer, and sat at the bar. One of the wait staff set a tray down next to him, picking up beers to go along with the steaming cups of coffee and – chai?

That's when it hit him. Chai. Keelan. City Hall. It was *Keelan* who'd bumped into him that day at City Hall. Keelan who'd made drop his new contractor's license in a pool of chai.

He'd called his new boss a 'bloody wanker'.

A surge of bile rose in his throat, and Peter gulped the water the bartender had just brought over to wash it back down. He quickly ordered a hamburger, and pulled out his wallet. As the bartender turned away, he hastily added, "To go, please."

Safely back in his room, Peter went through the texts from earlier, when he'd saved the contact in his phone. He didn't want to ask Keelan straight out if he'd recognized him, but he just had to know! Peter decided to send an innocuous text about site clearing and foundation work.

It was a grueling twenty minutes before he heard back. *Sorry for the delay, but was driving. Thanks for the update. I'll be at my father's firm the next few days. The new crew trailer will be there tomorrow, if you could be there to assist. Layte will be there and give you keys. Have a good night.*

Good. *Good.* Maybe Keelan hadn't figured it out. And Peter sure as hell wasn't going to bring it up. Portland seemed like a cool city, and he didn't feel like picking up and moving just yet.

CHAPTER 5

KEELAN SPENT the next few days focusing on projects for his father's company, and taking advantage of the long summer evenings to check out the jobsite before going home. He was pleased to see how much progress there had been on the cleanup. The teams must have worked overtime, because there was next to none of the concrete and waste that had been there when they bought it. They'd even started making some of the the markings.

Just before he got back in his car, his cellphone dinged. A text from Peter. *Would you have time tomorrow to meet and go over a few things?*

Before he could give it much thought, Keelan typed out *Sure*, and followed it up with "*9am?*

Brilliant! See you then.

Keelan had been so busy getting the last few

projects of his father's tied up and turned over, that he'd mostly been able to keep Peter Larkins out of his thoughts. Being holed up at his father's office had certainly helped. "Out of sight, out of mind," he muttered as he started the car.

After the drive home and a quick dinner, Keelan settled in for the night. It was in the low 80s, so he stripped to his boxers, turned on the ceiling fan, and opened the French doors that took up most of his bedroom wall. Eight floors up, the hustle and bustle of the streets sounded sort of like faraway surf. Occasionally, though, the cheery 'ding-ding' of a streetcar reminded him that there was a city below. He climbed into bed, the cool bamboo sheets against his nipples jolting a happy sensation down to his core. He palmed himself through his boxers and let his imagination run.

Keelan wasn't much for porn. He liked it okay, but that wasn't what he used when he allowed himself to 'blow off steam' as he called it, thinking that sounded so much less clinical than 'masturbation'. It also didn't make him sound quite so desperate for another man's touch.

It had been *far* too long.

An image of well-defined arms popped into his head as he gave himself a squeeze, and hello –something was definitely happening. The arms filled in with broad shoulders and a sculpted chest covered in clipped hair. He imagined a slender waist with a dark treasure trail leading down tight abdominals and beyond the belly button. Further down to more closely cropped hair framing a thick, magnificent cock. The vivid image made Keelan throw one arm over his face and bite at the muscle. He groaned as the fantasy man in his head reached for his dick with sturdy, experienced hands.

Keelan spread his legs, pressing his cock through his boxers, then dragged his fingers over his balls, sending a shiver up his spine. As his fingers pushed further, grazing over the sensitive skin just below his balls, he pictured more of his fantasy man, suddenly seeing on a strong chin. Sharp cheekbones. And hot, wanting, deep brown eyes.

He moaned as the image became clearer, then stilled. There was something familiar...

Keelan's eyes shot open and he sat straight up in bed. He knew that face; he'd been trying to forget it for days. And he knew those eyes the color of nutmeg.

Peter Larkins.

Keelan righted his boxers, any desire to blow off steam tonight having fled. Even though he hadn't intended to, he still felt slightly dirty for thinking of Peter in that context. He was an employee. Even if he wasn't, Keelan couldn't see them together, because they were two *very different* people.

Keelan took a deep, frustrated breath, then sighed gustily. He flopped back down and turned on his side, stared out the French doors for a while, and then closed his eyes in an effort to put the day behind him.

Sleep didn't come for hours. When it finally did, it was haunted by dreams of dark eyes that watched him in the night.

*
* *

Keelan parked his car and waved at a backhoe operator that he'd known for years. Though Portland was growing by leaps and bounds, some communities still felt small and construction was one of them. He checked in with the team leads about the new break trailer, happy to hear that it was a big hit with the men and women working. Besides truly wanting to keep the crew happy, it helped strengthen his reputation as a good boss, which could give him an edge when there were more jobs than teams, and crews chose employers instead of the other way around.

After checking a few other things around the site, Keelan walked in the office and found Peter standing in front of the pinned up plans, next to a desk buried with paperwork. Layte said that he'd been busy, and Keelan can see that clearly in the progress that was being made outside. But in here, it looked like controlled chaos. He wondered if that was how Peter usually worked – not that he was complaining. He wouldn't micromanage how things got done as long the job was on (or ahead of) schedule.

Peter turned at the sound of the door, and smiled. It showcased the laugh lines next to his eyes, and gave Keelan a warm feeling. "Keelan! I'm glad you could come in today."

Keelan couldn't help but smile back, even as he fought the blush he could feel starting. It was powered by the images his mind had conjured up last night, and it didn't help that Peter's shirt was open at the collar, and showed a glimpse of chest hair.

His imagination had been accurate. Dammit.

"Good morning," he said, putting his phone and keys on his desk. "Looks like things are going rather well out there."

"We're only half a day ahead of schedule, but the project is still in its infancy. Give me a few weeks and we'll be so far ahead that you can take your time with the finishing details instead of being rushed."

Peter had confidence in abundance. But, some-how, he didn't seem cocky.

"I've got a few questions, if we could walk around the property. Is this a good time?"

Keelan was nearly to the door when Peter stopped him with a hand on his shoulder.

"One second." Peter grabbed his clipboard, and added, "Don't forget this." He gave Keelan a hard hat, their hands touching for longer than strictly necessary. Keelan had to admit that it sent a thrill down his spine. "At least your hair's short enough it won't get too messed up by one of these," he said, donning his own hard hat with a wink.

Keelan's mouth went dry at the sight of Peter's sexy wink. Rather than risk squeaking if he tried to talk, he turned and walked out into the cloudless Portland morning.

Peter had no idea why he kept touching Keelan. It was like his hands had a mind of their own. Even when he tried holding his clipboard with both hands, he still ended up touching Keelan's shoulder or arm to direct him to areas that he had questions about. Being 'touchy-feely', as he'd heard it called, wasn't who he was. For one thing, it was extremely un-British. But for some reason, Keelan made him disregard the habits of a lifetime.

It wasn't *just* that Keelan was so attractive. Peter had been with plenty of beautiful people, and never reacted like this. There was something *different* about Keelan, though Peter couldn't pin it down. This reaction was also new, and something he wasn't used to. It made him want to follow Keelan, like the moon follows the Earth.

Even though he couldn't articulate why, feeling Keelan's delts or biceps flex beneath his rusty red shirt left Peter half hard. Thank goodness he'd grabbed his clipboard for their walk around the jobsite!

"And the last thing is over there." He turned Keelan by the shoulder towards the back of the site. They walked in silence to the only structure still standing on the property.

"Oh, Jacob's house," Keelan said with the first genuine smile Peter had seen him give. He was obviously fond of this Jacob, whoever he was.

Peter pulled out a key and unlocked the door, pushing it open and gesturing Keelan inside. "After you."

The house was musty, having been closed up for who knows how long. Dust layered every surface, including what little furniture remained. The décor and fittings obviously hadn't been updated in decades, but there was something about it that felt quite homely to him.

"Jacob Hart is who sold Layte and me the property," Keelan said as he looked around. "Mr. and Mrs. Hart were a big part of this neighborhood for years. I played in the vacant lot almost every day, and spent the majority of every summer vacation there. We all did. And we made sure to come here for trick or treat *every* year, 'cause Mrs. Hart made the best caramel apples."

"Did they die?"

He didn't mean to make him sad, but Keelan's expression fell instantly. "No. Well, *she* did. Mrs. Hart. But Jacob sold us the property so he could go live with his son in Eugene."

"What are you planning on doing with the house?"

Keelan looked at the built-ins and faded wallpaper. "I'm not sure. I know we turn the lot into overflow parking or a retention pond. But... There's something here I just don't want to let go of." His shook his head – maybe he couldn't believe he was prioritizing sentiment over business?

Peter smiled, encouraged that his idea might work. "So, how about I take it off your hands?" Keelan's gaze flew up to meet Peter's. "Not, you know, *buy* it. But rent it? That way, I'd be right here when any issues pop up."

"You'd have to get furniture," Keelan said, then added, "But you don't have to rent it. Just pay for utilities, and it's yours."

"Thanks," he said, reaching out shake on it.

Keelan hesitated for the briefest of moments. Peter's smile grew as he felt Keelan's warm hand enveloping his own, and made himself let go sooner than he'd have liked.

"Layte can give you the details on service providers," Keelan said. "And you might want to air the place out before you move in."

"Thanks, Boss," Peter said as they left. Locking the door, he added, "I'll hit up Craigslist to find stuff. Hey, should I get a couple extra beds, in case you or Layte need to stay onsite?" Dammit. He hadn't *meant* that to sound so suggestive.

A slightly panicked expression flashed across Keelan's face, but was quickly replaced by a cool professional demeanor. "No, but thanks. Layte lives nearby, and my parents are just a couple blocks over."

"Brilliant," Peter said, to cover his disappointment.

CHAPTER 6

DAYS AND WEEKS sailed by as they made rapid progress on the project. As the summer days stretched out in seemingly endless hours of sunlight, Keelan stayed at the jobsite later and later. He justified it as being available to coordinate and troubleshoot, but most often found himself talking to Peter late into the evening. Peter, who had worked throughout Britain, and traveled all over the world. Most of his travels had been for fun, though he alluded to less pleasant reasons, like being shipped off to boarding school by an emotionally absent father so someone else could deal with his problems.

Keelan knew that being abandoned by *both* parents bouncing from foster home to group home was no easier than Peter's childhood. He might have been sent away for school, but at least he had a home to go when the term ended. Still, Keelan felt lucky, because he'd been adopted by the Greenes and found what young Peter had craved; a stable home and people to love and care for him.

Staying late after the workday ended soon became the norm, and Layte left a stash of snacks for the inevitable late nights. She stayed for some, but usually left after the crew left for the day. Keelan's mother even stopped by with leftovers on several occasions, saying, "Your father and I are never going to be able to eat all this."

"Then why did you make so much, Mom?" Keelan would tease as Peter tucked into whatever delicious meal she'd brought.

His mother would just smile and pat his cheek, always leaving thereafter.

After a scorcher of a day, made even hotter by the asphalt that had been laid throughout the site, the fans in the office couldn't keep up. Keelan stretched and flapped the front of his shirt, enjoying the extra airflow. He was focused on the next day's plans when Peter got up to look in the treats drawer, his linen shirt outlining the muscles of his back. After a moment, he made a discontented noise.

"What's up?"

"Cupboard's bare." Peter absently scratched his stomach, which immediately drew Keelan's gaze.

He'd tried his best to remain strictly professional, but the lean lines of Peter's physique still made him think extremely unprofessional thoughts.

"Oh, yeah." Keelan cleared his throat. This time his voice didn't crack. "Layte said she's got a bunch of stuff to bring in tomorrow."

"Doesn't help us tonight," Peter said as he closed the cabinet and went back to his desk.

Keelan went back to his plans, even as his back complained that he'd been hunched over all day.

Some time later, Peter broke the silence. "How 'bout I make you dinner?"

Keelan straightened up so fast that he practically fell out of his chair.

"Well?" Peter said. "You *do* need to eat, yes?"

Keelan's stomach chose that moment to announce its agreement by gurgling. Loudly.

"I guess I could eat," Keelan said, trying to sound nonchalant.

Peter's smile was huge. "Steaks okay? I've got a couple marinating, and I've been meaning to break out the grill I got last week."

Keelan's stomach growled again.

Peter laughed. "Sounds like yes to me! Give me twenty minutes, then come round to the house. Deal?"

Keelan just nodded, in case his voice decided to

break again. Once Peter was gone, Keelan buried his head in his hands. It was just dinner with a colleague, right? That's all it was – that's all it *could* be. Except that the longer he worked with Peter, the deeper his desire seemed to be. As well as trying to stay professional, he'd been protecting himself, because Peter seemed to be the exact opposite of what Keelan was looking for. Well, *would be* looking for, *if* he was looking. *Which he wasn't.*

Trying to distract himself, Keelan started reviewing things he and Peter had already gone over that week: what permits were needed, which approvals were outstanding, and what the next phase would be. He studied them so thoroughly he almost had them memorized. When he jumped in surprise as his phone dinged, he realized that the distraction had worked.

It was a picture of Peter, standing over a grill and holding a bottle of wine. *Hope you like red!* He jumped again when another text arrived. *Just about ready, come on through.*

Keelan took a deep breath as he stood up, trying to ignore the partial chub he sported because of *those eyes.* Peter's dark eyes were so inviting that they made Keelan want more. More than he should be willing to take and, possibly, more than Peter was willing to give.

Closing up now. Be right there.

With the flick of a few light switches and a twisting of the key, Keelan stepped out and followed the scent of a grill toward his future.

Keelan hadn't been back to the house since offering it to Peter. The first thing he noticed was that the lonely emptiness that had filled it since Jacob left was gone. It had been a home when the Harts lived there, but the vacant house was just a hollow shell. Now it held a recliner and mismatched couch with a fuzzy throw draped along the back, and there were stacks of books on the coffee table. Peter must be an avid reader, another thing that endeared him to Keelan. In the kitchen, a small table and chairs sat in just about the same spot where the Hart's had been.

"Out here!" Peter called.

Keelan turned to go outside and nearly tripped at the sight of Peter, standing at the grill in a tight white tank that showed off his broad back and well-defined arms.

Keelan was in trouble. The semi he managed to talk down on the walk over here was suddenly straining his pants again, and that was before Peter bent over to set the grill cover on the brick patio. Keelan stutter-stepped through the sliding glass door as Peter took the steaks off the grill.

"Perfect timing!" he said, handing him the platter. "Can you take these inside?"

Keelan nearly dropped the food because he was focused on Peter's arms. He'd known Peter worked out regularly because of their discussions, but his dress shirts hadn't led Keelan to expect anything like *this*. Free of his button downs, Peter well-defined biceps were covered with a light sheen of sweat and nearly mesmerized him.

It took a second for Keelan to react, saying, "Yeah, sure." He tried not to lean in when Peter gave a quick squeeze of his bicep before turning to go inside. Keelan followed, wondering when Peter's dress slacks got so tight? Or had he just never noticed how well-shaped Peter's butt was? He stepped into the kitchen as Peter was grabbing a container from the refrigerator.

"Anywhere's fine," Peter said. "I just need to finish this."

Keelan set the platter on the table as the aroma of sautéed mushrooms and earthy spices filled the kitchen.

"Hope you like mushrooms," Peter said, tilting the cast iron skillet to show its contents. Keelan was more focused on his bicep as it flexed in the sunlight pouring through the windows.

Keelan's mouth was watering, but only about 40% because of the food.

"Sit, sit," Peter said, gesturing with the skillet. "Unless you'd rather eat outside?"

Keelan took a moment to consider, but the overhead fan tipped the balance.

"Cooler in here," he said, sitting at the table. He looked at his hands, ordering them not to reach out and pull Peter to him. He glanced around to keep from staring at Peter and the bottle of wine from the text caught his eye.

"Want me to open this?" he asked as he picked it up. Willamette Valley Pinot Noir. A good choice.

Peter opened a drawer, and tossed the corkscrew to Keelan and nodded at the pass-through. "Glasses are over there."

After making quick work of the cork, Keelan poured them each a glass. He leaned against the counter where he had a view of the kitchen and the living room. As he idly swirled the dark ruby wine, he looked over both rooms.

"You've really spruced it up nicely," he said. There was the furniture, of course, but also lots of artwork on the walls, both prints and paintings. Either Peter had found the most artistic Craigslist sellers ever, or he'd gotten them at the Portland

Saturday Market, which he'd recently discovered, courtesy of Layte.

Instead of responding, Peter placed a bowl of salad on the table and took the steaks to the stove.

"Have you decided what you're going to do?" Peter asked. When Keelan looked confused, he added, "With this place. The house."

"Not really, no. Why?"

As he plated the steaks and spooned mushrooms over them, Peter nodded to the sliding door. "Surveyors were marking up the yard, and leaving boundary stakes. There're also marker flags for the underground utilities." He set the plates on the table and gestured for Keelan to take a seat. "Like they're getting ready to demolish it or something."

Peter's voice was strained, and Keelan hurried to reassure him.

"No, no," Keelan said as he took his seat. He noticed that his feet were quite close to Peter's and that made him nervous for some reason.

"Cheers," Peter said. Keelan looked up to see Peter holding out his glass, so he picked up his own, and they clinked them together.

"Cheers." He took a sip. The wine was deep, trailing the slightest burn down his throat while the strong plum flavor and hints of pepper and earth danced along his taste buds.

"They must have been doing some additional markings. We have too many good memories of the Harts to just knock it down."

"*Good.*" Peter nudged Keelan's foot under the table. It was just a light touch, but it sent a jolt up his leg. "Because you'd have to evict me first."

Peter's statement made Keelan study him for what seemed an eternity. "What do you mean?"

Peter took a bite of his steak and looked around. Keelan followed his lead, careful to include some of the mushroom sauce. The hand-stenciled design around the pass-through again caught his eye.

Peter spoke quietly, but passionately. "I can't explain it, but something about this place brings me comfort. Like the whole house is giving me a warm, happy hug."

A spark of hope ignited in Keelan's chest. This certainly wasn't the wanderlust-filled guy he'd first met. He took a sip of wine to give himself a moment to think.

"Really? So, what brought that on, Mister World Traveler?"

"Honestly? I don't know."

Keelan studied him, catching the faraway look in his eyes.

"Like I say, it's this place. Not just this house, but Portland, too. It just," Peter locked eyes with Keelan as he continued, "feels *right*." After a sip of wine, he added, "I've never really wanted to settle down anywhere. Buy a house, set down roots, stay forever. But if I did, I think Portland is where I'd like to do it."

Something broke in Keelan, like a wall giving way and setting loose all the feelings he'd been trying to corral. He stood up and held out his hand, pulling Peter to his feet when he took it. Keelan rested his hands on Peter's hips and watched him nervously lick his lips.

"Can I?" he whispered.

Peter is ahead of him, caressing his face with calloused fingers before leaning in for a kiss. Keelan felt Peter's slightly chapped lips gliding across his – chastely at first, until he pulled back and bit at Keelan's lower lip. Keelan's lips parted and he drew in Peter's tongue. They both groaned as he pulled Peter even closer and deepened the kiss.

They shut out the rest of the world as their tongues danced and their hands explored each other. When Keelan pulled back, he looked into dark eyes heavy with want, and rested his forehead against Peter's, not wanting the moment to end.

*
* *

Peter wasn't sure what just happened. Why

Keelan was suddenly pulling him up and clutching at his waist with slim but strong hands. He stopped worrying about it when his lips connected with Keelan's and he licked his way into his warm and silky mouth. It felt like his world was finally starting to make sense after all these years.

Peter looked into Keelan's expressive green eyes and felt like he was falling. They felt warm and comforting, but also stirred something so deep in him that it was a little uncomfortable. He ran a finger over kiss-bruised lip, eliciting a moan. When Keelan took his hand, a spark passed between them that stole his breath away. His already racing pulse quickened even more.

Peter glanced down the hallway that led to the rest of the house, then gave Keelan an inquiring look. He smiled as Keelan blushed deeply, but nodded. Abandoning their dinner, he led Keelan to the bedroom he'd claimed and kicked the door shut, even though they were alone.

Once inside, Peter released Keelan's hand to deal with his vest, making quick work of it. He then had to watch as Keelan, maddeningly slowly, unbuttoned and removed his own shirt and vest. He couldn't resist the acres of gorgeous olive skin before him and reached out to caress Keelan's pebbled nipples. The resultant moan made his prick swell, and he quietly vowed to inspire Keelan to make that sound as often as possible.

Peter backed Keelan into the lowboy dresser he'd picked up from Freecycle, then lifted him onto it so they were nearly the same height. Keelan groaned at the manhandling, and Peter surged forward to try and taste it on his lips. He meant to flick Keelan's nipples but got distracted when Keelan groped him through his trousers, derailing all coherent thought.

Keelan's hand slipped inside his waistband, hot against his throbbing cock. Peter buried his groans in Keelan's neck, licking at the sheen of sweat, and then biting as he chased the musk and warmth he found there.

"Peter." Keelan sounded desperate, but when Peter checked, he saw only beautiful pools of green that he'd imagined getting lost in too many times to count.

Peter ducked his head and ran his tongue over Keelan's pulse point. He grinned when it broke out in gooseflesh, then leaned back, and again sought out those intensely green eyes. "Can I take you to bed?"

"*Yes, please,*" Keelan answered. He wrapped his free hand around the nape of Peter's neck and pulled him into another searing kiss.

Peter worked his hands back under Keelan's strong thighs. He might be taller, but Peter had a good two stone on him, and all of it was muscle. Keelan yelped when he picked him up, but then growled as Peter lowered him to sit on the edge of the bed. The growl sounded anything but angry, and he smiled down at Keelan. "You really like that, don't you?"

Keelan's blush said everything his mouth didn't. Peter's smile grew because it was another piece of the puzzle that was Keelan. Peter wanted to know all his pieces, so he could take him apart and then put him back together again.

Taking a step back, Peter whipped his belt from its loops and dropped it on the floor. He pushed his trousers and pants down while he toed off his shoes, and then kicked the whole tangled mess under the bed. Before he could work on undressing Keelan, he'd leaned forward and started licking and kissing Peter's abs. Then his hand encircled Peter's cock, pulling back the foreskin and running a thumb along his slit.

"Oh, god," Peter gasped, desperately sucking in air when Keelan drew him closer to rub his stubbled chin across the head. Peter was still shuddered at the sensation when Keelan pulled him in and slid his tongue over the sensitized skin.

"Keelan, look at me." Keelan's wide green eyes locked onto his as he continued sucking, twisting with his hand as he took Peter deep into his velvety warm mouth. "Keelan," he whined.

Just as the orgasm began to pool in his belly, Peter stepped back. Keelan released him with a quiet 'pop', but maintained his slow, deliberate strokes. Peter put his hands on Keelan's shoulders and laid him back on the bed so as to get him naked as fast as possible. He tossed trousers in one direction and pants in the other (where they landed on his desk, judging by the sound of scattering paper). He took a moment to look his fill, then licked his way into Keelan's mouth, pulling away a second later to lick his palm and take Keelan's shaft in a firm grip.

Keelan arched off the bed, so Peter pinned him with his weight and claimed his mouth again. Keelan's cock was hot in his hand, longer and skinnier than his own. Unlike most of his partners, Keelan was circumcised, and Peter was fascinated by the differences. He teased the slit with his thumbnail and watched it leak copious amounts of pre-come. Peter stuck the tip of his tongue in the slit and grinned when Keelan jolted like he'd been shocked.

Peter looked down at Keelan's lightly furred pecs, then along the tiny trail that darkened just below his belly button until it disappeared into his thatch of pubic hair. He bent down and licked a pebbled nipple while jerking once, twice, and then loosening his grip before dragging his fingernails over Keelan's balls. They were tight and responsive, just like Keelan's body as it writhed under each lick and stroke Peter tried.

Peter lifted Keelan's balls, heavy and warm in his palm, until he could stroke the silky skin behind them. He glanced up and found Keelan looking at him hungrily, so he let a fingertip dance around his hole. Keelan moaned so deep in his chest that Peter felt it instead of hearing it.

"Is this okay?" he asked, punctuating the question with rhythmic pulses of his fingertip.

Keelan groaned again, but Peter swooped in and swallowed most of it. Keelan planted both feet flat on the bed to give Peter better access, which he immediately took advantage of.

"Will you fuck me?" Keelan's voice was thready, tinged with desperation.

Peter wanted nothing more.

"One second." He claimed another kiss before getting up and going to the desk. He'd picked up condoms and lube with his groceries last night, and hadn't put them in the nightstand yet. A quick rummage got him what he needed and he tossed the rest back where he'd found it, sending more papers fluttering to the floor. He turned around to see

Keelan smirking at him, and hurried back to kiss it right off his face.

When Keelan looked stunned instead of smirky, Peter used his teeth to open the security wrap on the lube and toss it away. He pulled out a condom, dropped it on the bed, and laid back down, mostly on Keelan. As he licked into his mouth, his lubed fingers slid past Keelan's testicles, and he reveled in the sounds Keelan made as one finger breached him. Warm. Tight. He slowly pushed deeper, intoxicated by Keelan's reactions.

When he added a second finger, Keelan moaned in pleasure and clutched his arm. Peter watched Keelan's expressions as he changed the angles, and slipped in a third finger when it hit 'bliss'. He was almost in a trance when Keelan took a deep breath and said, "I'm ready. Fuck me."

Peter almost hated to stop, but couldn't resist Keelan's request. He kissed him and grabbed the condom, licking his way down Keelan's body until he had to stand up or fall off the bed. He put his hands on Keelan's waist with a grin, then slowly pulled him to the very edge of the bed.

He lifted those long, lean legs up onto his shoulders and then nestled his prick atop Keelan's before opening the condom. He winked at Keelan's incredulous look. "I wanted you to have a good view." He made sure to stroke his knuckles along the underside of Keelan's dick as he rolled on the condom and then applied the lube.

Peter slid backward until his head was teasing Keelan's waiting hole. He pushed in closer, then retreated. And again. A third time. He leaned down to gently bite Keelan's lower lip, then captured his mouth and swallowed the deep sigh that escaped as he breached the tight ring. Keelan's arms encircled him, and held on tight. Peter froze, and they stayed like that until Keelan let out a cross between a moan and a whimper, and then loosened his grip.

Keelan nodded and dropped his legs from Peter's shoulders to around his waist. Peter braced his arms on the bed and pushed in slowly – ever so slowly. Maddeningly slowly until he was completely buried in Keelan's tight ass. He froze again as Keelan shifted, then pulled out and paused. Keelan's heels digging into his back prompted him to resume.

Peter started thrusting slowly, but picked up the pace at Keelan's pleading, until his hips were pistoning in and out, going deeper with every stroke. Each time Peter hit his prostate, Keelan's whimpers grew. When Keelan's started panting in short, ragged bursts, Peter knew he was getting close.

"Can you come for me, baby?"

Keelan just kept urging him on with his powerful

legs. Peter leaned in for another kiss, and then stood up, unwrapping Keelan's legs from around his waist and draping them over his elbows, so he had full access to Keelan's ass, and Keelan could jerk his weeping cock. Keelan matched his pace at first, but then sped up and threw his other arm over his eyes.

"No, baby – let me see you. Let me watch you come," Peter said.

Peter loved watching Keelan teeter on the edge as he shifted his hips to target his prostate. Their eyes locked again as Keelan's face contorted in ecstasy, and his ass clamped down on Peter. His hand was a blur, and he spilled his seed with a powerful cry, letting it paint their bodies where it landed.

Fuck. That was one of the hottest things Peter had ever seen. He let go of Keelan's legs, pulled out and stripped off the condom with a practiced movement. He jerked his dick, once, twice, and then gave himself over to one of the most powerful orgasms he'd ever experienced. His come was painted along Keelan's neck. His chest. His belly. The final two jets spattered across his groin, and filled Peter with a primal satisfaction. He took one last pull, letting the head drag across the coarse hairs of Keelan's balls, and collapsed beside him on the bed.

The day had been unbearably warm, and the

heat pouring off them now threatened to melt them into the bed.

"You're amazing," Peter said, when he finally caught his breath.

Keelan opened his mouth, but closed it without saying anything. Instead, he smiled as a blush crept up from his neck. How could someone look so debauched and completely bashful at the same time?

They touched and kissed for what seemed hours, neither moving to get out of bed. When Keelan started to sit up, Peter put an arm out to stop him. "Stay?"

Keelan smiled. "I should clean up, at least."

"Okay, but then stay the night." Peter let him go, and they ended up sitting on the edge of the bed.

A somewhat strained silence followed, until Keelan took Peter's hand and stood up.

"Shower?"

Peter gratefully accepted. They kissed while the water got hot, and kept breaking into entranced smiles as they soaped each other up. After they dried off and brushed their teeth, Peter led Keelan back to the bed and climbed in behind him. He didn't usually sleep with his bed partners, and didn't spoon them on the rare occasions that he did, but holding Keelan felt *right*. As he pulled Keelan even closer, he felt whole. Complete. For the first time in his life.

It was like he'd been craving this, but didn't realize until he got it. He'd come to care so much, so quickly, that it scared him. He wanted to ask if Keelan felt the same, but didn't want to frighten him off. So instead, he just whispered, "Goodnight," into the shell of Keelan's ear.

Keelan, his smile limned by the last glow of sunset, twisted around to kiss Peter.

"Goodnight."

CHAPTER 7

KEELAN WOKE UP SLOWLY, his sluggish mind eventually realizing that he wasn't in his own bedroom. And he wasn't alone – someone had a possessive arm around his waist. It was the same someone who'd left beard burn on his cheeks and thighs.

Peter.

Last night's events flooded back, and he felt himself smiling helplessly, because it had been *so right*. Sure, a niggling doubt was worming around in the back of his mind, but he stomped it down. He didn't want anything intruding on their afterglow.

Well, it would be *their* afterglow if one of them weren't still asleep. Keelan turned over and looked at Peter. Without the stresses of running the project, he looked even younger than his years. His slight smile made Keelan want to wake him up, so they could start spending the day together.

Keelan brushed a kiss against Peter's cheek, but he didn't stir. Hm. He smacked a second kiss on the same spot, to test how heavily he was sleeping. Still no response, so he wiggled out of Peter's grasp and went to use bathroom. He was a bit stiff and sore from their escapades last night, but everything had loosened up the time he finished his ablutions. Peter was obviously out for the count, so Keelan figured he'd get dressed and go clean up their abandoned dinner. Then, maybe cook Peter breakfast.

That wasn't pushing too fast, was it?

Keelan found his shirt and pants, but his boxers seemed to have vanished. He finally found them by the desk, half hidden in a bunch of construction plans. Keelan picked them up, and caught a glimpse of a site name. His blood ran cold when he realized it wasn't for the business park.

He grabbed the rest of the printouts off the floor, and then looked through the ones on the desk. They were from all over the country, some with start dates a year or two out. Most had comments in Peter's impeccable handwriting, noting possible issues or regional temperature ranges. Several had 'Apply?' crossed out and 'Applied,' noted. Next to the papers was a folder with copies of Peter's project portfolio and resume.

Keelan first took the buzzing sound to be his heartbeat pounding in his head, but it turned out to be Peter's phone. The lock screen was lit up with a text.

Hey, fuckboi wanna stop by b4 work? Could use some more of that D

Keelan's heart dropped and he was suddenly as tense as piano wire.

The phone buzzed again.

Come on. Like you say its just sex, rite?

If Keelan had eaten dinner, he'd be throwing up right now. How could he be so stupid? How could he have given in? Thought that Peter actually cared about him? *Its just sex.* God, he was an idiot!

Keelan grabbed his clothes and shoes and ran out of the bedroom. Just before he stepped out on the porch, he realized he was still naked. "Dammit," he muttered, shutting the door and jerking his boxers on. He was so angry with himself he nearly toppled over trying to get his pants on. Not bothering to tie his shoes, he rushed out to his car and sped away, betrayal burrowing deep into his chest.

CHAPTER 8

PETER'S PHONE alarm woke him from a delectable dream, but the memory of last night was even better. He didn't care that it had been less than a day – he *knew* they could be something special together. Peter liked who he was with Keelan, and he wanted to pursue that and never let it go. It felt *right*, even as his father's voice echoed menacingly in his memory, "Never sleep with the boss."

"Keelan?" He grabbed his phone and silenced the alarm. The sheets were cool, but maybe he'd needed the toilet. Peter tried again as he got up. "*Keelan?*"

Still no reply, so he checked the toilet and then went out to the kitchen, but Keelan was nowhere to be seen. He felt a pang of uneasiness, but then figured that Keelan had probably headed to the office already. They'd laughed about him being more of a morning person than Peter, and how that was a very low bar. He unlocked his phone to call Keelan and saw he had a couple of texts.

'Hey, fuckboi wanna stop by b4 work again? Could use some of that D'

'Come on. Like you say its just sex, rite?'

Normally he'd be all over that because the guy was a hell of a lay. But after what he'd shared with Keelan, 'Blueshirt Glasses Guy' held no interest for him, and neither did his lewd invitation.

Sorry. Think I'm off the market. Ta.

There, that should do it, but he could always block the number if need be.

Peter clicked over and hit Keelan's contact. It rang. Then rang some more. When it finally picked up, it went straight to voicemail.

That was odd.

Maybe he was in the shower, or talking to one of the construction crews. No matter. Peter sent him a quick text.

Hey, beautiful. Be there soon.

Peter cleared away their abandoned dinner before heading off to shower and get ready for work.

*
* *

Three days. It had been three days and Peter had heard *nothing* from Keelan, other than a one-word text that said, *"Sorry."* He felt like someone had drained all the color out of his world.

"Watching his desk will not bring him back any sooner, Peter," Layte said, over the whir of the fans.

Peter hadn't realized that he'd been staring again. Layte raised an eyebrow and looked pointedly at his mouth. *Dammit!* He yanked the pencil out of his mouth and saw that he'd chewed nearly the entire length. "Sorry," he muttered, going back to staring blindly at the plans on his desk. After less than a minute, he stood up and stretched. "Maybe I should make the rounds again."

"You just returned from *rounds* ten minutes ago," Layte reminded him kindly. "Perhaps you should go home and have lunch. Or take the rest of the afternoon to rest? Try and get your mind off–" She shot a glance at Keelan's desk. "Other things."

Though Layte was born in Oregon and had only been out of the country twice, her precise diction and pronunciation often led people to think she came from elsewhere. And her non-traditional college and career path gave her a wealth of experience to share. Talking with her usually felt like being friends with a UN ambassador. It was normally quite soothing.

Now, though, Keelan's absence left an ache in his chest that nothing could ease.

"Have you heard from him?"

Layte glanced away. "Perhaps he just needs some time."

Peter knew that she and Keelan were best friends, and wondered if he'd said something to her.

"I hate this." He leaned back and dug the heels of his hands into his burning eyes. He needed to get out of this stifling room beats. If he was going to be sad and frustrated, he could at least be out where there was a *chance* of a breeze. "I'll be back in a bit."

He saw Layte nod as he walked out of the trailer.

As he aimlessly rounded another corner, memories from *that* night played over and over in his mind. He'd never felt so connected with another man, but maybe it hadn't meant as much to Keelan. Maybe to him, it *was* 'just sex'. God, wouldn't that be ironic, considering how many guys Peter had fobbed off with that line. He didn't want to believe that, but maybe Keelan was a better actor than he seemed.

Peter glanced at his watch and realized it was nearly 4pm. Most of the crew should already be gone, what with the even earlier start times now that building erection had begun. Only the laborers would be left, cleaning up the site to prep it for tomorrow. He sighed, then turned and slowly made his way back.

After two blocks of watching his feet trudge their way toward the office, Peter almost tripped when he looked up to see Keelan's car in the small lot. His eyes flew over to the trailer and found Keelan standing at the door, staring at him with angry green eyes that seemed to be trying to bore right through him.

CHAPTER 9

KEELAN COULDN'T TELL which of them was more shocked. He'd been standing on the porch for at least a minute, psyching himself up to face Peter in the office. Having him walk into the parking lot made Keelan feel trapped, even though they were outside and 15 or 20 feet apart.

Peter opened his mouth, but Keelan just nodded at him before hurrying inside and closing the door.

"Keelan," Layte said, sounding concerned.

Keelan had just set his satchel on the desk when they heard thunderous footfalls on the metal steps, and the door flew open. Peter stood in the doorway, looking completely unlike the confident man of last week.

"Keelan?"

"Sorry. I'm sorry for disappearing like that, but

my father needed me at the firm. I, um," he paused, glancing at Peter, "had some things to deal with."

"Of that I have no doubt," Layte said. "But I was under the impression that most of your father's employees were off. Was not the annual 'closing of the office' this week?"

Keelan's face felt like it was on fire. As his best friend, Layte always called him out on his bullshit whether they were alone or in public. He should have talked to her before running off, but he'd needed time to piece his tattered pride back together. And to construct a façade he could hide behind in order to survive being around Peter.

The silence hung heavy until Layte stood up so quickly that her chair rebounded off the wall and into her legs.

"Keelan, I am grateful that you're back. Quite a few things need our attention, and I would be most unhappy if you disappear like that again." She nodded toward Peter as she continued. "However, I believe the most important situation awaits you right here. We can go over the remaining items in the morning."

She gathered her things and fixed Keelan with an intense look when she reached the door. "I expect this to be dealt with by then. Understood?" Without waiting for an answer, she sidestepped Peter and left.

Keelan nodded his head, but avoided looking at Peter. He couldn't. Not yet.

Another long silence stretched out between them. Keelan sighed and dropped into his chair, happy that Peter's desk was the farthest one away. (Not that it was very far at all, but he was still glad for the small favor.)

"Keelan," Peter said as he closed the door. "Would you talk to me?"

Keelan ignored the pleading in his voice, even though it tugged at his heart. He focused on removing several cardboard tubes, each with an updated plan for one of their buildings, out of his satchel.

"Keelan," Peter repeated, reaching out as he approached Keelan's desk. Keelan wasn't ready for any sort of physical contact, so he hurriedly placed two tubes into Peter's extended hand.

"Here." He knew he sounded cold, but he'd split that first day between crying and railing at himself about being taken for a fool. Then he'd spent the next two building a wall around his heart, so he could finish the project – even if it meant working with Peter until it was complete.

A sneering voice in the back of his mind whispered, 'Until he leaves. *He always leaves.*'

"Are you fucking kidding me?" Peter's voice went from pleading to spitting fire.

Keelan had never heard Peter speak like that. Sure, he'd lambasted the subcontractors who'd wasted two days and thousands of dollars after someone turned the plans the wrong way up. But this venomous tone was downright hateful.

Peter dropped the tubes, crossed his arms over his chest, and glared down at Keelan from across the desk. After visibly counting to ten under his breath, Peter took a deep breath and uncrossed his arms.

"I'm trying to talk to you, Keelan," Peter said, more evenly. "We had an incredible night together-"

Keelan snorted in disbelief.

Peter's expression said that Keelan might as well have slapped him. Keelan shook his head as he looked Peter up and down, wondering what he was still trying to sell when he'd already gotten what he wanted.

The silence grew oppressive, like the heat before a thunderstorm broke.

"So that's it, then," Peter finally said.

Keelan had spent a long time figuring out exactly what to say to Peter, the man who had broken down his defenses to reach his wary heart – and then ripped it out of his chest, like it was nothing more than a game. He finally met Peter's eyes.

"It's just sex. Right?"

Keelan was very relieved his voice didn't waver. He hadn't been sure he would even be able to speak around the lump in his throat. That same lump made it hard to breathe as he held Peter's coal-dark eyes, not backing down until Peter closed them. Winning that particular match meant he could walk away with *some* dignity. After approximately an eternity, Peter raised a hand to wipe the sweat off his face and then spun on his heel.

He stomped to his desk, making the windows rattle. He grabbed his phone and backpack and stormed to the door, where he paused, looking like he was searching for the right words, but only said, "Ta." Then, with a slam that once again rattled the windows, he was gone.

Keelan gusted out a sigh, dropping his elbows on the desk to bury his face in his hands. He sat there in the overwhelming heat, accompanied only the whir of the fans, for what felt like an hour.

If he'd won, why the hell did it feel like he'd just lost everything?

CHAPTER 10

KEELAN ABANDONED the trailer after a long, frustrating session of accomplishing exactly nothing. Every time he started to make any progress, he'd see Peter's empty chair in the corner of his eye. The office, which once held so many good memories, now did nothing but frustrate him. He knew he shouldn't have come back yet, but there were things he needed to go over with Layte. Plus, he'd hoped it was late enough in the day that Peter would be gone.

Keelan left the site, obsessing about the mangled situation with Peter. As he pulled onto the Banfield freeway and found it at a complete standstill, his frustration rose even higher. Late evenings in the trailer had meant that Keelan drove home with very little traffic. Now, with traffic going nowhere and the heat threatening to overcome the air conditioning, all he could do was stew.

It took over or an hour to get across the river, but as soon as he was able, he got off and took surface streets to his condo. He pulled into his parking space, snatched his satchel, and slammed the door before stomping over to the elevator.

"*Of course,*" he growled as he found an Out Of Order sign waiting there. And seeing as how he was on the top floor, he now had eight stories to trudge up. "*Nine,*" he muttered to himself, since the garage was one floor underground.

Once he was finally in his apartment, huffing and out of breath, he stood in front of a vent for ages. He only moved to grab a tall glass of water and guzzle it down standing at the sink. Normally, he would enjoy the sensation of coolness pooling in his belly. Tonight it only stirred up the sourness that had plagued him since he'd left Peter's.

He opened the refrigerator and looked over the meager selection, hearing his father saying, "*You never eat enough.*" It wasn't *his* fault he was lean. Hell, Keelan literally translated into 'lean one', so he was just living up to his birth name, right?

Acid burned the back of his throat at the thought of eating, so Keelan shut the door and took a couple antacid tablets instead. He sat on the couch and clicked through channel after channel, but there was nothing on to distract him from what had happened last week.

He sat up at the sound of a deep voice with an accent identical to Peter's, but then shook his head and shut off the British nature program. He fought the urge to throw the remote against the wall, but finally tossed it in the corner of the sofa. And even though it was barely 7 P.M., Keelan got up to take a shower and head to bed.

The tepid shower helped his sore muscles a bit, but did nothing about his mood. After drying off, he put on a pair of sleep shorts, grabbed his phone, and crawled under the sheet.

Keelan opened the texting application and stared at Peter's name, before scrolling to Layte's contact and hitting it. *Hey.* When she didn't respond after a minute, he dropped the phone on the bed, fell back on his pillow, and scrubbed his face with his hands.

He replayed the events of the last week over and over, just like he had countless times since that day. He knew that he'd drawn away from everyone, but he needed to protect himself, right? As he picked up his phone again, he realized he'd cut Layte out, too.

One reason he'd been so hesitant to date was

having seen too many people lose touch with their greater circle of friends through being completely wrapped up in their romance. He'd never wanted to do that to Layte, and yet he had anyway. First, because everything with Peter had been so brand new – and then because the aftermath had hurt like hell.

He startled when the phone rang in his hands, and accepted once he saw that it was Layte calling.

"Layte. Hey."

She said nothing for the longest time, then sighed. When she spoke, there was something off in her tone. *"Hello, Keelan. How are things with you? I felt it would be better to call. Especially given the circumstances."*

Circumstances.

"I'm sorry?"

Keelan realized that he'd said it out loud.

"Sorry, sorry," he said. "I'm just..." He wasn't sure *what* he was at the moment. Angry. Tired. Frustrated. Heartbroken. No, he couldn't be heartbroken over a man he barely knew. Sure, he'd come to like Peter over the past few weeks, but he was nothing more than a transient. He had no roots. Nothing planned beyond his next project. No meaningful attachments of any king. And worst of all, no foundation to start a life with anyone. "I don't know *how* I am, to be honest."

"*Hmm. I don't know what happened between you and Peter-*" At Keelan's sharp intake of breath, she quickly added, "*and I don't need to know, because that is your business. But I think you should consider very carefully before you do anything rash.*"

Layte was right, of course. Layte was *always* right.

Keelan's grip on the phone tightened. "I know," he whispered. "It's just so hard, you know?"

"*And who said love is so easy that any fool can fall into it, hm?*"

Keelan smiled for what felt the first time in years. "Thank you, Layte." He could practically hear her smile on the other side of the line.

"*Will I see you in the office in the morning?*"

He paused for only half a second. "Yes, you will. Bright and early."

"*Goodnight, my friend.*"

Keelan felt lighter than he had all week. He plugged his phone in on the nightstand, then grabbed the book he'd been reading off and on for weeks. But as he read, the conversation with Layte kept percolating in his mind. She would see him in the office in the morning. *She.* Would it only be her in the office?

Or would Peter be there, too, to give him a chance to try and salvage what they could of their friendship.

The night dragged, and the uneasy feeling in Keelan's chest deepened. By the time he fell into a fitful sleep, he was practically back to that morning in Peter's kitchen. The morning where he felt like he'd lost part of his soul.

CHAPTER 11

KEELAN STUMBLED TO THE BATHROOM, unsurprised to see bags under his eyes. He'd barely slept the night before, and every time he managed to nod off, he'd been haunted by dreams of being abandoned. Not just by Peter, but his birth parents, friends, and family.

He routed an upbeat playlist through the condo's speaker system as a distraction while he shaved. He planned on making an overture to Peter that might at least salvage their friendship. It probably wouldn't be exactly what it had been, but Keelan was willing to do what he had to in order to move forward. For the project's sake and Layte, if nothing else.

He filled his largest travel mug with coffee and a couple shots of espresso, then drove across the city to the jobsite. Avoiding rush hour traffic was half the reason he liked construction's early start time, plus it was good to be on site to handle the issues that regularly came up. He had to admit, though, that the other half was spending more time with Peter.

Traffic had slowed by the time he approached the exit. And his coffee was down to dregs by the time he pulled into their lot. No matter; he could get a refill in the office. Peter somehow produced the best coffee out of their rinky-dink coffeemaker.

He shook his head as he pulled into a parking spot, looking up in surprise as Layte pulled in right behind him. He got out of the car, grabbing his satchel and slinging the strap over his shoulder as he waved to her. She smiled, but looked worried.

"Good morning, sunshine!" Keelan said, hoping to get a genuine smile out of her.

"Good morning, my friend," she replied. But her smile was still strained, and she seemed down.

"What got you out of bed so early?" He caught her up in a warm hug that helped ease some of the tension he'd been carrying. In his bones, though, Keelan knew that the only way to deal with the turmoil in the pit of his stomach was to make things right with Peter.

"I wanted to be here for you," she replied, her eyes warm and caring. It was one of the things he loved most about her. No matter what, she always kept Keelan honest, and comforted him in times of need. Keelan knew that today would absolutely be one of those times.

They walked over to the trailer stairs, where Keelan gave a rakish gesture. "After you, madam."

Layte studied him for a moment as she pulled out her key. She climbed the steps and opened the door, nodding for him to precede her. He complied, but could feel that something was different. The entire trailer felt *off*.

Layte put her things down, then surprised Keelan by taking a seat on the edge of his desk, blocking his view of most of the trailer.

"What's going on?"

"Why don't you tell me?" She studied him with compassionate eyes.

Keelan took a deep breath, letting it out as an unhappy sigh. He dropped his hands in his lap and picked at his cuticles. They both knew it was a stalling tactic, but Layte let him get away with it for nearly a minute. Once she cleared her throat, Keelan knew he had to come clean.

"I didn't mean for anything to happen," he finally said. "I mean, you know me, Layte." He braced himself to look into her eyes.

"I know you very well, Keelan. And I know that you deserve to be happy. As does Peter."

Keelan couldn't help but flinch at Peter's name, and knew that Layte had seen it.

"I also know you two finally got over this silly dance you were doing and did something about it. You made each other happy – if only for a fleeting moment."

"That's just it," Keelan confessed. "It was amazing. I *was* happy."

"You *both* were," Layte said.

"But how could I ever be with someone like that? Someone who has no connection to his past? Someone who goes from place to place, held there only by the job. And when he's done with the job, he just..." Keelan waved his hands to convey how unsettled he felt. *"He just leaves!"* After a few shaky breaths, he looked at Layte, knowing he had tears welling up in the corners of his eyes. "I feel so close to him, Layte." He gestured toward Peter's desk. "I don't know if I can handle it if he..."

Keelan's voice trailed off as he focused on Peter's desk. It was clean. Not just tidy, but cleared off. No more sticky notes. No collection of reusable cups from the many coffee shops in the neighborhood. No picture of Peter and his father. Everything had been removed except the blueprint tubes, markers and pencils, and a blueprint of the project on the wall behind his desk.

"Peter and I spoke last night just before you texted me," Layte said. "He thought it would be best if he stepped aside. Last night, he reached out to Samuel Edgecomb to see if he could take over the project. Sam turned it down, but he gave Peter a list of people he would trust to finish the project."

Keelan felt like the air had been ripped from his lungs, and a cold chill ran down his spine. "So he's leaving me?"

He grimaced when he realized that he said 'leaving *me*' instead of '*leaving*.'

"Indeed. We had a long talk about the situation. Though he hates the thought of leaving, he felt it would be best for all involved." Layte went and got a piece of paper from her desk, then set it in front of Keelan. "These are the project managers he thinks would be best to step in for him."

"But how could he do this?"

"He didn't want to," Layte replied. "But, given the circumstances, he felt he had no choice."

"Maybe it's a choice for him, but it feels like a part of my soul's been torn away." He jumped up and starting pacing. "I never realized, but I didn't truly feel whole until I met Peter. Until I *kissed him*. Leaving him that morning was the hardest thing I've ever had to do. But I *had to*."

Layte watched him for a long, uncomfortable moment.

"Keelan, do you remember when I told you that you had to find your true self? And you found your truth deep within you?"

Keelan stopped in his tracks, thrown by the question. Why was she bringing it up now? When it became clear she wouldn't continue until he replied, he said, "Yes. That was when I came out to you."

"And why did you come out to me?"

"Because I needed to be honest with myself. And I needed to share that truth with you, because it made me feel better about myself. It made me feel-" He stopped, considering his next words carefully. "Whole. It made me feel *whole*."

"And did you do that because you *had to*?"

"No. I did it because it was the right thing. For me."

And there was her smile.

"Now tell me this." She tossed her hair over one shoulder before continuing, "The situation with Peter. Did you walk away from it because you *had to*? Or because it was the right thing to do *for you*?"

Keelan slumped onto the edge of his desk and buried his face in his hands, choking back the saddest of laughs. "How did you get so smart?" He scrubbed his face with both hands and looked up at her.

"It is not me who is smart. You are the one who realized that what's best for you isn't following the path you were intended to, but rather the path your heart leads you on."

"But what if he breaks my heart?"

Layte nodded. "That is a possibility. But what if you never offer him your heart in the first place? You know that Peter will love you back if you take that leap, because he already does."

She studied him briefly. "I know you feel that tradition is the most important thing. But there's nothing to say that you and Peter can't start traditions of your own. And from that foundation, your love can grow stronger, together."

Layte was right. He *knew* she was right. He also knew that before anything else, he had to make things right with Peter. He stood up, feeling more hopeful than he had in days. "I need to get over there."

Layte glanced at her watch. "Yes, you do. He's booked on a flight in two and a half hours."

The blood drained from Keelan's face. He had to go – *now*. If he didn't, he might miss out on his one chance at life. At love. But as he grabbed the door-knob a cold feeling rolled over him. What if Peter wouldn't listen to him? What if Peter wouldn't even let him in the door? After all, Keelan had been the one to leave.

"What is it?" Layte asked. "You must go. *Now*."

"What if he doesn't want to talk to me? What if he won't even let me in? I mean, he has every reason to hate me now."

Layte looked pensive for a moment, before breaking into her sunniest smile. "I have an idea," she said, jangling her keys.

CHAPTER 12

PETER TOOK THE 'KEEP PORTLAND WEIRD' fob off his key ring and wound the house key onto it. He dropped it in his pocket and looked around the house. He was leaving a few pieces of furniture and art that he'd picked up where they sat. He told himself they were too bulky to transport, but, really, he just wanted a clean break from Portland. Wanted to start over, again.

"It's what you do, Petey boy," he muttered, forcing a smile. Inside, he was completely miserable.

Trying not to dwell on it, he opened the ride-sharing app he'd been using to get around. It made no sense to get a car when he worked less than a block away. Almost anything he needed was within walking distance, and for everything thing else there was public transport and letting someone else drive him. Besides, not paying for a car increased what he could put into savings. Good thing, too, since he'd have to dip into them now that he was leaving the project before its completion.

Peter clicked over to contacts, his thumb hovering over Keelan's name as memories of their time together ran through his head. But the more he thought about it, the angrier and more unhappy he became. He'd wanted to fight for Keelan – for *them*. But since Keelan wouldn't even give them a chance, he knew it was best to just walk away.

With a heavy sigh, Peter hit the "Edit" button. He tried not to think as he punched the "Delete Contact" option. Keelan's contact disappeared as a stabbing pain seemed to puncture his heart. "What's done is done."

Peter fought the urge to throw his phone into the wall, knowing that the satisfaction of watching it shatter just like his heart had, wouldn't last. Instead, he sent it to sleep and tucked in his pocket, pulling out the keychain and dropping it on the table.

He sat in silence until a car announced itself by crunching over the gravel driveway. Peter took a deep breath as anger and sadness raged within him, then let his fingers glide over the ancient key.

"So much for Portland."

He rapped his knuckles against the table as he

stood up, then grabbed his suitcase, and opened the door. Setting his suitcases on the porch, he turned for one last look at walls and linoleum that have seen more life than he can imagine.

"Goodbye, Keelan," Peter whispered, locking the door. His voice broke, but had to tell the truth for once instead of simply running away. "I will miss you. More than I ever thought possible."

The deadbolt snicked shut, closing that chapter of his life. Suddenly the world felt a little colder, even as the heat of the day enveloped him.

With heavy steps, Peter walked to the car and rapped his knuckles on the trunk, which popped open obediently. He put in his two suitcases, then threw his backpack over one shoulder as he opened the rear door and got in.

"Would you like to sit up front?"

He knew that voice.

Peter's head shot up and he looked into beautiful green eyes he'd given his soul to a few nights ago. Though he'd been hurt and angry before, he felt his heart breaking. "Keelan?"

Keelan smiled at him. It felt warm and healing, even as Peter wondered where the catch was. At his wary expression, Keelan's smile faded, and he turned away. It tore at Peter's heart to see him wipe away the tears that had welled up.

They didn't speak for what felt like hours. Keelan cautiously broke the silence. "I'm here to take you to the airport, if that's okay. Or Layte will – if, if you don't want- But I'd really like a chance to talk to you."

Peter's throat was too tight with emotions to say anything. He got out of the car and Keelan followed suit, meeting him at the trunk. Keelan reached out to lay his palm against Peter's cheek, then pulled him in for a barely-there kiss before resting their foreheads together.

"I'm so sorry. I saw those other projects and thought you were leaving. I didn't want to get in any deeper, so I tried to walk away. I was stupid, and-"

Peter wrapped his arms around Keelan's waist, pulling him close and tracing his fingers across skin that he'd mapped with his fingers, his tongue.

"It's okay," he said, and then kissed Keelan. And again. They started out chastely, but became more passionate as Peter used his lips, his tongue, and his teeth to tell Keelan what he couldn't otherwise say.

Peter pulled back, then surged forward for one last kiss to banish Keelan's remorseful expression.

"Well, pop the boot, you," he said, once he'd caught his breath. Before Keelan could get to the key, Peter had a realization. "*Bugger*! I locked the keys in the house!"

Keelan smiled and let let out a relieved laugh, then rewarded Peter with the smile he wanted to wake up to for the rest of his life. Keelan gave him a mischievous look as he jangled the keychain. "It's a good thing Layte has a spare."

Peter couldn't help but kiss him again.

EPILOGUE

Epilogue (10 months later)

It had taken Keelan a little while to get used to waking up here, but the warmth and weight of Peter by his side was imminently familiar now. He looked around the room at the enlarged windows and the walk-in closet they'd added to accommodate two grown men's wardrobes, and smiled.

He'd loved his high-rise condo in the Pearl, but keeping the Hart's house standing had appealed to him. And now that they'd completed the modernization, he and Peter had settled into the old house together. Now, he came from work every night truly feeling like he was coming *home*, instead of just the place where he slept.

Peter's fingers slipped up and down his belly as light as a feather and his husky whisper tickled

Keelan's ear, "Morning, love." Keelan could feel Peter's hardness against his back.

"Morning," Keelan said, pushing the covers off them both and turning in the muscular arms that encircled him. He leaned in and kissed Peter as one of hand reached under the covers and tugged lightly at Peter's cock. "Is this for me?"

"Long term lease," Peter smirked, adding, "with an option to buy."

And they would do it, one day. They'd get married. Once the business park was up and running, and his father retired and left them in charge of the firm. That was a little ways off, but they had time. As he looked into Peter's eyes, Keelan thought, 'We have the rest of our lives.'

He shivered as Peter captured his mouth and ran calloused hands up and down his spine. "Love you," he said, resting his cheek against Peter's for a moment. Then, quick as a whip, he let go of Peter's dick and gave him a playful smack on the bottom. "Busy morning ahead," he said, taking advantage of Peter's outrage to scoot out of bed. He reached out his hand. "Come on, sleepy head. We've got a lot to do."

Peter sighed, then took Keelan hand and brought it to his lips to kiss the inside of his wrist. While

Keelan still was smiling at him fondly, he hauled him back into bed.

"I just need ten more minutes," Peter said through a jaw-cracking yawn.

"Only ten?! Gonna need at least twenty to make it worth my while." They shared a laugh, then Peter rolled them over so Keelan was stretched out next to him. He lifted Keelan's leg and started kissing from his ankle down. "Oh, *hello*," Keelan said. Just as he was relaxing into the thought of fooling around and possibly being late, Peter nipped the back of his knee and hopped up.

"Light snogging and maybe a jobby in the shower?"

Peter *loved* the shower they'd put in, as evidenced by the number of times they messed around in there.

Keelan stood up, faked Peter out with a kiss, and raced for the bathroom. He got there first, then leaned against the doorframe and ran one hand down his stomach. "Better hurry up or I'll start without you."

Peter nearly left little cartoon dust swirls coming to join him.

*
* *

Today was the big day. Today they'd be opening Hart's Square. Businesses had been moving in over the last couple of weeks, but none were officially open yet. Most of their tenants were coming, and several would be participating, but Layte and Keelan had flown Jacob Hart up from Eugene to perform the ceremonial ribbon cutting.

Keelan and Peter arrived at the Hart's Square maintenance office an hour before the scheduled start, walking into a room full of people talking convivially.

"We're here," Keelan announced. "Wow, I didn't think there'd be so many."

"There were others," Layte said as she greeted them each with a kiss to the cheek. "However, they grew tired of waiting for you two."

Wait, was that a knowing smirk? Had Layte guessed why they'd been delayed? He hoped not, but wouldn't put money on it. She seemed to know everything.

"And so they decided to go and check on their units. They will be back in thirty minutes, along with the press."

"The press, wow," Peter said.

"Well, this *is* one of the largest business park projects in Portland's history," Layte said. "You *were* aware of that, Peter, were you not?"

Peter laughed. Of *course* he knew it. But Layte loved to tease him, just as she teased Keelan.

Then there were hands to shake, people to greet, and far too many names to learn. Still, Keelan attempted to 'press the flesh' as Peter called it, of as many people as he could until Layte said that it was time.

Peter, ever the organizer, had arranged an area for the press, another for attendees' families, and even a dais so everyone would be able to see the ribbon cutting.

There were at least a hundred people either taking part or watching, including Keelan's parents, most of the construction crew, and their first tenant, an older man starting up a scientific firm. Smack dab in the middle of it all was Jacob Hart, with his son and daughter-in-law at his side.

Layte and Keelan each spoke about what the land and the project meant to them, and then waved for Jacob to come say a few words.

"What? Me?" he'd asked, but stepped up next to them and turned to the waiting crowd.

"My Lucy and I held on to this property for years because we never felt it was the right time to sell. Then, not five minutes after I put up the sign, Layte and Keelan came over to talk about their plans. Looking at all these brand spanking new buildings around us, I'm sure it was the right decision. Lucy would have thought all of this was just great.

"To Layte and Keelan, I wish you nothing but success. And may you both be as happy on this land as my Lucy and I were for over sixty years."

The crowd gave a tremendous cheer, along with applause and a couple of piercing whistles.

Jacob Hart took the scissors and held them over the ceremonial ribbon.

"May you all be as blessed as we were, and do wonderful, meaningful things with your lives. Here's to a wonderful future for us all." With that, he snipped the ribbon cleanly in half.

Keelan reached for Peter's hand. "To a wonderful future, my love."

ABOUT THE AUTHORS

Walter is an emerging author who has published in multiple genres. This is his fourth book.

Lisa is Walter's longtime writing partner of self-published fiction. This is her second book.

When they aren't writing, they're usually either talking on the phone about writing, or feeding their voracious appetites for reading.

ADDITIONAL WORKS

ALSO BY WALTER HOPGOOD AND LISA D. WITTE

A Million Miles Amok: A Guidebook For The New Road Warrior

Hart's Square: Foundations of Love

Hart's Square - A.I. Think I Love You - Coming Soon!

ALSO BY WALTER HOPGOOD

Migration: Beginnings

Migration: Knowledge